The Diaries of Robin's Travels

D1638177

Sweet Cherry
Publishing

Published by Sweet Cherry Publishing Limited
Unit E, Vulcan Business Complex
Vulcan Road
Leicester, LE5 3EB
United Kingdom

www.sweetcherrypublishing.com

First published in the UK in 2016
ISBN: 978-1-78226-250-3
© Ken Lake 2016
Illustrations © Creative Books
Illustrated by Vishnu Madhav

The Diaries of Robin's Travels: Istanbul

Printed and Bound by Wai Man Book Binding (China) Ltd,
Kowloon, H.K.

Istanbul

ISTANBUL

ANKARA

BURSA

IZMIR

KONYA

ANTALYA

ADANA

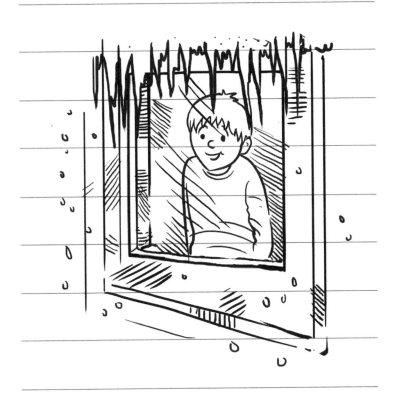

Robin was awake early. He opened his bedroom curtains and looked out at a cold and frosty street. He was glad he didn't have to go to school in this weather! The street glistened with ice.

Mrs Woodhouse was taking her dog, Wobbler, for a walk. He seemed to be having a few problems with his feet. As he tried to move them forwards, they went sideways. Then all four legs spread out on the ice and he landed on his big belly. He couldn't move at all! Mrs Woodhouse tried to pull him up, but then her legs went out of control too and she slipped off of her feet and landed in the middle of the street next to Wobbler.

Mr Brown saw what was happening and went to help. He tried to pull Mrs Woodhouse get to her feet, but it was so slippery that he fell down as well!

The postman, who had seen all of this happening, tried to help too. It was no use, though. He fell down and lots of letters started falling out of his

big, red postbag and blowing down the street.

Robin had found this quite funny, but he wasn't

sure what to do. He called Mum.

"What can we do, Mum?"

"There's only one thing for it, we will have to call the fire brigade!"

So that's what she did. The fire engine soon arrived with bells ringing and blue lights flashing.

"Oh no, I should've known Wobbler would be involved again! Is anybody injured?" the fire chief asked.

The postman had a bruised bottom but that was all, so there was no need to call an ambulance. Then the fire brigade got everybody back on their feet and sent them home. It took four of them to lift Wobbler!

"What have you been feeding him?" the fire chief

asked. "He's very heavy!"

"Oh, well he really likes his cheese," Mrs

Woodhouse blushed.

"I'm sure he does. I think he needs to go on a diet!"

The postman picked up his letters and very carefully got on with his deliveries. Robin decided he should call Grandad and tell him all about the disaster of the frosty morning and the icy street.

Ring, ring, ring, ring!

"Hello Grandad, you will never believe what has been happening in the street!"

"Did it involve the fire brigade?" Grandad chuckled.

"Yes, how did you know?"

"Oh, I just guessed."

Then Robin told him all about it. Grandad laughed.

"Anyway, Robin, how was your week at school?"

"Well, in geography our teacher, Mrs Clements, has been talking about the **continents**. It's quite confusing, I'm still not sure where **Europe** ends and **Asia** begins!"

"That's a tricky one, Robin," Grandad said.

"Can you explain it, Grandad?"

"Well, it's quite fascinating really, Robin," he began. "Many millions of years ago, all of the land masses and continents on earth were joined together. This land mass was called **Pangea** **[pan-gee-ya]**. Then, about two hundred million years ago, the land slowly started to drift apart to form separate continents. Now we have **North America**, **South America**, Asia, **Australasia**, **Africa**, Europe and **Antarctica**."

"What about the North Pole, Grandad?"

"No the **Arctic** isn't a continent; it's a huge sheet of ice floating on the sea."

"So there are seven continents in all? But how do you know that they used to be joined together? I'm sure even you can't remember that far back!"

"Quite right! If you look at a map of the world you will see the continents can fit together like a giant jigsaw puzzle. Have you got a map of the world in front of you?"

"I'm afraid not, Grandad."

"Well in that case, I'd better bring mine over for you!"

Robin put the phone down and went to wait at the front window.

Beep, beep, beep, beep!

Grandad's little red car turned onto the street.

"Alright Robin, let's have a look at my map of the world."

Grandad spread it out on the kitchen table.

"Look, can you see that if we could slide the continents around, they would all fit together?"

"Wow, that's amazing! So they were once all joined together and called Pangea?"

"That's right Robin, and now they have all drifted apart."

"Miss Clements has asked us to find out about the country **Turkey** over this weekend. She said it spreads over two continents, is that true?" Robin asked.

"Yes. There is a city in Turkey called **Istanbul**, and it is known as the **Transcontinental City** because it spans across two continents: Europe and Asia."

"So, is Turkey the place our Christmas dinner comes from?" Robin asked.

"No," Grandad chuckled. "The Christmas birds

originally came from North America."

"Oh right. Well, can you tell me a bit more about

Turkey?" Robin said.

"I can do something better than that, Robin. How about we go there and see the country for ourselves?"

"That sounds incredible!" Robin grinned. "Thanks, Grandad."

For the whole of the next week, Robin couldn't talk or think about anything else other than his trip to Turkey. Thankfully, the time went by quickly, and before long he and Grandad were waiting at the airport. They heard a crackly voice on the public address system:

"The Turkish Airlines flight to Istanbul is now boarding at gate seventeen."

Soon they were on the plane and heading

for Istanbul.

"How long will the flight take?"

"Less than four hours."

"I can't wait! What will we see when we get there?"

"Well Robin, Istanbul is where east meets west. That includes religions and cultures." Grandad pulled his travel map from his pocket and pointed to the city.

"The city is right on the **Bosphorus [bos-fer-us] Strait**, that's the piece of sea which joins the **Black Sea** and the **Marmara Sea**. It also separates Europe from Asia, or at least the part of Asia which used to be called Asia Minor."

Grandad showed Robin the different places he

spoke about on the map.

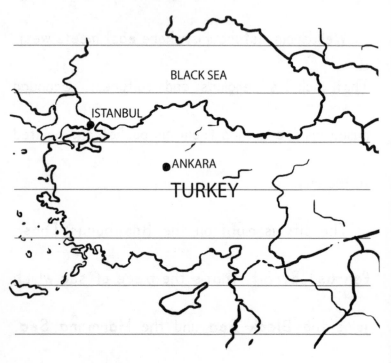

"So, is Istanbul the capital of Turkey?" he asked.

"No, Robin, the capital of Turkey is **Ankara** which

is more or less in the middle of the country, and at

the centre of the **Anatolian [an-a-tow-lee-an]**

Peninsula. Istanbul is the largest city, though."

They were soon airborne and Robin chattered

non-stop all through the flight.

"What sort of money will we need?"

"The currency is the **Turkish Lira**, but most places will take Euros."

"And what about visas like we had for **Russia**?"

"I have got those as well. They are valid for ninety days."

Soon they had landed in Turkey, and were soaking up the fascinating sights and smells.

"It's not as warm as I thought it would be, Grandad!" Robin was glad he had brought a jumper with him.

"Well it's winter here, Robin, just like it is at home. It's much hotter in summer."

Grandad hailed a taxi, which took them into the busy city centre. Robin clicked his camera to take a photo.

"Wow, this looks like a very interesting place. What shall we see first?" Robin said.

"I think we should ask the magic book," Grandad replied.

Grandad carefully took the little book out of his pocket, held out his hands, took a deep breath and cast his spell.

Little book, make it so,

Tell us all we need to know,

People, places, countries, towns,

Show the jewels in all these crowns!

Then something wonderful happened. The book flipped open to a picture of a beautiful mosque; then it began to shake and sparkling dust burst from the pages. Suddenly, from out of this glittering cloud, there appeared a little man no bigger than Grandad's finger. He was smartly dressed in a suit and wore a necktie, a clean white shirt and the tallest hat they had ever seen. Robin and Grandad were speechless as they stared in wonder. He stretched and yawned, then spoke to them.

"Hello! Thank you for waking me up. Who are you?"

"I'm Robin and this is Grandad," said Robin.

"But . . . who are you?"

"Well, Grandad and Robin, I am called **Mustafa Kemal Ataturk** and I am credited with founding modern Turkey back in 1923. Welcome to the wonderful city of Istanbul!"

"Thank you very much, Mr Ataturk, where shall we start?"

Robin looked around. There were people everywhere, as well as cars and bicycles. He looked up and saw many skyscrapers reaching up into the blue sky.

"Well, there is so much to see here," Mr Ataturk rubbed his chin. "There is architecture from many different historical periods. But I think we should begin with the **Blue Mosque**. Everybody has to see it!"

"Err, could you tell me what a mosque is?" Robin said quietly and frowned.

"Of course, Robin, it's a holy building in the **Muslim religion**. It's a place where Muslims go to pray. It's a bit like the churches in the Christian religion."

"Oh, I see," Robin nodded.

"This is one of the very few in the world with six minarets."

"What are minarets, Mr Ataturk?"

"Minarets are tall towers used for the call to prayer. In the Muslim religion it is customary to pray five times a day."

They stopped a taxi which drove them close to the Blue Mosque.

"We are in the **old quarter** now," Mr Ataturk smiled. "Can you see that mass of water over there?"

He pointed. Robin and Grandad both looked and could just see, in the distance, sparkling blue water

"That is the Bosphorus strait."

"Wow! It's beautiful." Robin said. "Grandad has told me all about it."

"It forms part of the boundary between Europe and Asia. That is why they say Istanbul is where east meets west." Mr Ataturk said. "Now, let's go and see the mosque."

Mr Ataturk led them through the cobbled streets to a grey and white building. It had a domed roof and six thin towers.

"This beautiful mosque was designed by a Mr Aga in the Seventeenth Century. Please remove your shoes."

Grandad and Robin felt the floor under their feet and stared in wonder at the incredible sight.

"Why do we have to take our shoes off?" Robin asked, looking at his toes on the red and blue carpet.

"It shows respect, Robin," Grandad said. "It stops any dirt coming inside this beautiful place."

Mr Ataturk nodded and said that Grandad was right.

"This great building was built under the reign of **Sultan Ahmed the First**, so it's called The Sultan Ahmed Mosque. It's commonly known as The Blue

Mosque, though, because of the wonderful blue tiles on the inside walls."

"What's a **Sultan**?"

"A Sultan was the title for a noble ruler."

"I suppose you are going to tell me that his wife was a **Sultana**!"

"Yes, Robin, that's very clever. How did you know that?"

"I just guessed," Robin winked at Grandad who chuckled quietly.

As they walked through the wonderful building, sounds echoed from wall to wall. On the ceilings were patterns made from blue tiles, as well as grey, gold, red and white. There were large rings holding beautiful lights hanging above their heads.

Mr Ataturk then directed them into the big courtyard area, showed them the turrets on the corner domes and pointed out the shady arcades. Robin took lots of photos and Grandad scribbled down the information their guide had given them.

"Alright, let's get our shoes. If we go across a small park we can see the magnificent building called **Aya Sofya**, or sometimes known as Hagia Sophia."

"What is it?"

"Let's go and see!" Mr Ataturk chuckled.

From the outside, it was a little bit like the Blue Mosque except it looked more orange. There were also only four turrets and many more domed roofs.

As they walked in, it took their breath away. It was a huge and elaborately decorated building.

"Wow, Mr Ataturk, what is this place?"

"Aya Sofya is very old as you can see. This building dates back more than fifteen hundred years. It started out as a Greek **basilica [bas-il-ika]** or church, then became a mosque. It is now a museum."

"I can't believe it's so big!"

"Yes, you must see the glittering mosaics in the galleries upstairs."

Robin quickly took a few photos with his camera before they browsed the mosaics.

As they walked back outside into the sunshine, Grandad took out a new pencil. The old one was worn down to a little stub. Then Mr Ataturk asked

Robin a question.

"Tell me, Robin, do you know what a **Hamam** is?"

"Err," he thought for a moment, "I'm afraid I don't."

Grandad shrugged too.

"Well, the original meaning of this Arabic word

is a place of cleansing. But today it is used to

describe the public **Turkish Baths**."

"Baths?" Robin said. "But why didn't people have a bath at home?" He thought of his own big white tub, filled to the brim with bubbles.

"Baths haven't always been inside people's homes," Mr Ataturk replied. "In ancient times, people used public baths. The Romans used them too. It was a place to wash, get a massage, and meet friends for a chat and relax."

"How can you talk if you're in a bath tub?" Robin frowned.

"These type of baths aren't the little white things with feet. These are built like huge swimming pools, so talking was easy." Mr Ataturk smiled at Robin, who looked quite impressed.

"I can't wait to see one," he smiled.

Both Robin and Grandad were mesmerised by the incredible sight, neither of them had seen anything like it before.

"This is the **Ayasofya Hamam**."

"So, it is the Ayasofya baths?" Robin smiled.

"Quite right!" Mr Ataturk said loudly. "I'm pleased that you're learning."

Robin and Grandad enjoyed their time in the baths. It was calm and everybody was friendly.

"You two are quiet," Mr Ataturk winked as they were leaving.

"I'm just so relaxed," Robin sighed. "I wish we could do that more often!"

"Maybe you will get a chance to go again before you have to leave our lovely city."

"What shall we do next?" Grandad said.

"I'm hungry," Robin rubbed his tummy.

"Me too! What sort of food do you recommend, Mr Ataturk?"

"Well, Istanbul has lots to offer because of the many cultures here. But I would suggest that you try some of the kebabs."

"Yes, I have heard of kebabs: meat and vegetables cooked on long skewers."

"That's right. You should get a side dish of fruit as well. You will find melons, apricots, plums, apples, grapes, pears and lots of other fruit either fresh or dried."

Grandad and Robin found a little restaurant on one of the cobbled side streets.

They enjoyed the food that their guide had recommended, and washed it down with freshly squeezed pomegranate juice. Robin had apple tea to finish, whilst Grandad had a thick, dark Turkish coffee.

Then they found their hotel. They could hear the sound of the city through their window and smell all of the interesting spices and foods. They slept very well, mostly thanks to their soothing bath!

The next morning was bright and clear. Robin opened the curtains and looked across the street where he saw a big dog chasing a little cat. The little cat jumped up on a high wall and scowled at the dog.

Robin thought they looked like a Turkish Wobbler and Turkish Tiddles!

"What shall we see today, Robin?"

"We had better wake up Mr Ataturk and ask him."

So that's what they did.

"First I'm going to take you to see **The Grand Bazaar**."

"What's that?" Robin asked. He was excited.

"It's a large market, but unlike any you've ever seen before!" Mr Ataturk said.

He led them through the busy streets to the Bazaar.

It was full of colour. Everywhere Robin looked, he could see food, spices, fabrics and jewellery. He saw clothes, candlesticks, watches and clocks. They walked a little further on, and there he saw rugs, carpets and furniture. He couldn't believe his eyes!

"Wow!" he said. He clicked his camera at all of the different sights. "This is amazing!"

Mr Ataturk puffed his chest out in pride.

"This place has been in use as a trading area since 1461," he said. "Different Sultans have added buildings and made the site bigger over time."

They walked around for a little bit longer and inspected the items with big smiles. Robin was particularly impressed with the **Turkish delight**, which came in lots of different colours.

"What next, Mr Ataturk?" Robin asked.

Mr Ataturk stroked his beard.

"There's just so much to choose from," he said.

"I know! Let's see the **Basilica Cistern.**"

"Does the cistern have anything to do with water?" Grandad asked.

"Yes, it certainly did once. A cistern is a place to store water," Mr Ataturk replied. "This basilica was a huge water storage facility, one of many hundreds in Istanbul. In countries like England it rains a lot of the time, so there's plenty of drinking water. In countries with hot, dry climates like Turkey, it doesn't rain as much. This means that fresh water has to be brought up from rivers and stored."

So that is where they went next.

It was a magical moment when they stepped inside the cool building.

"This building was a central part of the system that once brought drinking water into Istanbul. It was originally constructed almost one thousand,

<u>five hundred years ago and then forgotten for</u>

<u>hundreds of years. The roof is supported by</u>

<u>three hundred and thirty six columns. Just look</u>

<u>at that one!"</u>

He pointed his tiny finger and they both stared, it was a column with a huge upside down head at its base.

"What an amazing sight! I can't wait to tell all of my friends and Mrs Clements."

"That's Medusa, Robin. Do you know who that is?" Mr Ataturk asked.

"I think so. You had better explain anyway."

"She is a figure from **Ancient Greek Mythology**. She has snakes for hair and if you look into her eyes, she will turn you to stone!"

Grandad and Robin quickly looked away, then they laughed.

"But why is there a Greek statue in Turkey?"

"Well, this beautiful country was once occupied by the **Ancient Greeks** and later by the **Ancient Romans**. They both built wonderful cities here."

"When did the Turkish people arrive, then?"

"The people we now call the Turkish were originally nomads from central Asia. They arrived here almost a thousand years ago and built around some of the great buildings that still exist. So you see, that is why there is such a mix of cultures and religions."

"I didn't realise that. So, what should we see next?"

"You absolutely must see the **Topkapi Palace**.

Make sure you have a sharp pencil, Grandad."

They soon stood looking at another beautiful building. It had domes and tall towers made of red, white, grey and blue stone. Robin took lots of photos.

"Please tell us about it, Mr Ataturk."

"What you are looking at here was the home for many generations of Sultans and their wives."

"Sultanas!"

"That's right, Robin. Look, there are lots of lush green courtyards and shaded seating areas. The family areas and especially the Turkish Baths are highly decorated with beautiful tiles. It has a large treasury too."

Grandad scribbled down a few more notes.

"Come on, let's walk around the palace."

So that's what they did. There were so many courtyards to wander through! They saw a building called the **Tiled Pavilion**. It had grey columns along the front, as well as dark blue tiled patterns.

"This is one of the oldest **Ottoman** structures in the city, built in 1472," Mr Ataturk smiled.

"Ottoman?" Robin frowned.

"Yes, Turkey was once part of the Ottoman Empire, along with many other lands including parts of **Southeastern Europe, Western Asia and Northern Africa**." Mr Ataturk stopped to check Grandad was keeping up with his notes. "It was named after Osman the First, who ruled a state in Anatolia."

"I recognise that word!" Robin said.

"That's because Anatolia is the centre of Turkey. That is where the capital, Ankara, is located."

Their legs were getting tired, and Grandad

looked at his watch.

"Mr Ataturk, we have to fly back to England

this evening. I don't think we have the time to see

anything else!"

"That's a shame! There are so many wonderful treasures here in Istanbul: there are many more mosques and the Archaeological Museum. That is where you can see an amazing display of scenes from **Alexander the Great**'s life. He was from Greece and created an empire that stretched across three continents!"

"We'll have to try and visit again one day!" Robin smiled.

Mr Ataturk then hopped back inside the little book. Robin and Grandad headed over to **Istanbul Ataturk Airport.**

"Grandad, this airport is named after Mr Ataturk!" Robin pointed to the sign above the doors. They both smiled as they thought of their tour guide.

Robin talked about Istanbul all through their journey home. He finally understood where all of the continents were, especially Europe and Asia.

When they arrived home, he got a big hug from Mum and Grandma.

"Welcome back, Robin, how was Turkey?" Mum said.

"It was absolutely delightful - and to prove it, I

have brought you both some Turkish delight."

   Robin winked at Grandad.

Want to know what Grandad's been scribbling in his notebook? Take another read through the book and note all the words in **bold** - you'll find out a little bit more about them!

Grandad's Notebook

Continents: The areas of land into which the world's suface is divided. There are seven continents in all.

Europe: The sixth largest of the seven world continents.

Asia: The largest and most highly populated of the seven world continents.

Pangea: A supercontinent that existed many millions of years ago. Two hundred million years ago it began to separate into the continents we know today.

North America: The third largest of the seven world continents.

South America: The fourth largest of the seven world continents.

Australasia: The smallest of the seven world continents.

Africa: The second largest of the seven world continents.

Antarctica: The fifth largest and least highly populated of the seven world continents.

Arctic: The region surrounding the North Pole.

Turkey: A country that spreads across the border between Europe and Asia. Most of Turkey is in Western Asia, but some of it is in Southeastern Europe.

Istanbul: The largest city in Turkey.

Transcontinental City: A city that exists on the border between two continents.

Bosphorus Strait: The piece of sea that separates Europe from Asia. It also connects the Black Sea and the Marmara Sea.

Black Sea: A sea in Southeastern Europe that drains into the Mediterranean. It is surrounded by six countries: Bulgaria, Romania, Ukraine, Russia, Georgia, and Turkey.

Marmara Sea: A sea in Turkey that connects the Black Sea to the Mediterranean.

Ankara: The capital city of Turkey.

Anatolian Peninsula: An area of land bordered by the Black Sea, the Marmara Sea, the Aegean Sea and the Mediterranean Sea.

Turkish Lira: The name of the currency used in Turkey.

Russia: The largest country in the world. It covers Northern Asia and most of Eastern Europe.

Mustafa Kemal Ataturk (1881 - 1938): The first President of Turkey and the founder of the Turkish Republic.

Blue Mosque: A famous mosque in Istanbul that is also known as the Sultan Ahmed Mosque. It is called the Blue Mosque because the inside is decorated with blue tiles.

Muslim religion: A religion also known as Islam, which follows the teachings of the prophet Mohammed.

old quarter: The oldest part of the city of Istanbul.

Sultan Ahmed the First (1590 - 1617): The Sultan of the Ottoman Empire between 1603 and 1617.

Sultan: The title given to a male noble ruler.

Sultana: The title given to a female noble ruler.

Aya Sofya: A famous historical building in Istanbul that is also known as Hagia Sophia. The building was first a Greek Basilica, then it was used as a mosque, and now it is a museum.

Basilica: A sort of church that has a central nave and aisles.

Hamam: The Turkish Baths.

Turkish Baths: A type of public bathhouse with steam-rooms.

Ayasofya Hamam: The Turkish Baths that are joined to the Aya Sofya.

The Grand Bazaar: One of the largest and oldest covered markets in the world.

Turkish delight: A popular soft Turkish sweet that is often flavoured with rosewater.

Basilica Cistern: The largest of the cisterns that exist beneath the city of Istanbul. Before being converted into a cistern it was a Basilica built by the Romans.

Ancient Greek Mythology: The stories that the Ancient Greeks told about their Gods.

Ancient Greeks (c. 800 B.C. - 500 A.D.): A civilisation whose influence spread from central Asia to the western end of the Mediterranean.

Ancient Romans (c. 500 B.C. - 500 A.D.): A civilisation whose empire spanned much of Europe, North Africa and the Near East.

Topkapi Palace: A large palace in Istanbul that was once home to the Sultans of the Ottoman Empire.

Tiled Pavilion: One of the buildings that make up the Topkapi Palace in Turkey. It is now a museum.

Ottoman (c. 1299 - 1922): An empire that, at its greatest extent, spanned much of Southeastern Europe, North Africa and the Near East.

Southeastern Europe: The area of land that lies to the south east of the European continent.

Western Asia: The area of land that covers the areas commonly known as the Middle East and the Near East.

Northern Africa: The northernmost region of Africa.

Alexander the Great (356 B.C. - 323 B.C.): An Ancient Greek king who ruled between 336 and 323 B.C. By the end of his rule, he had conquered an empire that stretched from the Adriatic Sea to the north-west of India.

Istanbul Ataturk Airport: Istanbul's main airport, and the biggest airport in Turkey.